Susie
the Sister
Fairy

Join the Rainbow Magic Reading Challenge!

Read the story and collect your fairy points to climb the
Reading Rainbow at the back of the book.

This book is worth 10 points.

To Lara and Isla, two very loving sisters.

Special thanks to
Rachel Elliot

ORCHARD BOOKS

First published in Great Britain in 2017 by The Watts Publishing Group

1 3 5 7 9 10 8 6 4 2

© 2017 Rainbow Magic Limited.
© 2017 HIT Entertainment Limited.
Illustrations © Orchard Books 2017

HiT entertainment

A CIP catalogue record for this book is available from the British Library.

ISBN 978 1 40834 508 5

Printed and bound in Great Britain by CPI Group (UK) Ltd, Croydon, CR0 4YY

MIX
Paper from
responsible sources
FSC® C104740

The paper and board used in this book are made from wood from responsible sources

Orchard Books
An imprint of Hachette Children's Group
Part of The Watts Publishing Group Limited
Carmelite House, 50 Victoria Embankment, London EC4Y 0DZ

An Hachette UK Company
www.hachette.co.uk
www.hachettechildrens.co.uk

Susie
the Sister
Fairy

by Daisy Meadows

ORCHARD

www.rainbowmagic.co.uk

Jack Frost's Spell

Of sisters I've just had enough.
And if you don't agree, then tough!
I'll steal the Sister Fairy's things.
Just watch the trouble my theft brings!

I'll get the Rainbow sisters too,
For my revenge is overdue.
Sisterly love will now be lost,
And all because of great Jack Frost!

The Dazzling
Diary Planner

Contents

Chapter One: Maple Cabin   11

Chapter Two: The Golden Trumpet   21

Chapter Three: A Shocking Surprise   31

Chapter Four: Gabbling Goblins   41

Chapter Five: The You-Know-What   51

Maple Cabin

The driveway of Golden Trumpet Adventure Camp was packed with cars.

"There's Kirsty," shouted Rachel Walker, jumping up and down as she saw her best friend's car drive up and park.

Kirsty Tate scrambled out of the back and dashed towards Rachel.

"I'm so excited
about this week I
can't stop thinking
about it," said
Kirsty as they
shared a hug. "I
even think about
it in my dreams."

"I can confirm
that she hasn't talked
about anything else for weeks," said Mrs
Tate, carrying Kirsty's rucksack over to
them. "I'm so glad that we saw the camp
advertised in the local newspaper."

"It was a brilliant idea, Mum," said
Kirsty.

Rachel and Kirsty hugged each other
again. Golden Trumpet Adventure Camp
was exactly halfway between their

homes in Wetherbury and Tippington. When Mrs Tate had suggested it, the girls had agreed that it was the perfect place to spend some time together.

Looking around, they saw a big wooden building behind them, with a big sign over the door.

**Golden Trumpet Adventure Camp
Dining Cabin and Offices**

A forest surrounded the dining cabin, and the sound of birdsong filled the air. A young man jogged over to them with a warm smile.

"Hi, I'm Tristan," he said. "I'm one of the camp leaders. It's our job to look after you while you're here and make sure you have a great time."

Rachel and Kirsty introduced
themselves and Tristan checked their
names on a list.

"You'll be staying in Maple Cabin,"
he said. "You will be sharing it with two
other girls, but they haven't arrived yet.
Follow me and I'll take you there."

The girls said goodbye to their parents,

picked up their rucksacks and followed Tristan into the leafy forest. The winding trail was so narrow that they had to walk in single file.

"The forest is full of trails like this," Tristan said. "This one is the quickest way from your cabin to the dining cabin."

"What sort of things will we be doing this week?" Rachel asked.

"Too many for me to remember," said Tristan with a grin. "There's horse-riding, waterskiing, hide-and-seek, obstacle courses, climbing, cycling – it's going to be great fun. Here we are – welcome to Maple Cabin."

He opened the door of a little log cabin with yellow curtains in the windows. Inside were two bunk beds, a table and four chairs. A thick, stripy rug was spread on the floor and there was a vase of flowers on the table.

"It's lovely and cosy," said Kirsty. "It'll be like having our own little house for a week."

"I'll leave you to get settled in," said Tristan. "I'll be back later to take you to the dining cabin."

As soon as the door closed behind him, Kirsty ran and jumped on to a top bunk. Laughing, Rachel put her rucksack down and sprang on to the bottom bunk.

"I'm looking forward to finding out who we're sharing with," she said.

"We'll have to be careful not to talk about fairies in our sleep," said Kirsty with a smile.

Rachel smiled too. She and Kirsty were good friends with many fairies, and they had visited Fairyland lots of times.

Just then, the cabin door opened and two girls walked in. The first looked about the same age as Rachel and Kirsty and had

long, chestnut-brown hair. The second
girl was about four years younger, but
she had the same chestnut-brown hair
and dimpled smile.

"You must be sisters," Rachel burst out.

"Yes, I'm Sarah and this is my little
sister Anna," said the older girl. "Isn't it
exciting to be at camp?"

The Golden Trumpet

The four girls chatted as they unpacked their things, and soon they were all giggling together.

"You two seem like really good friends," said Sarah.

"We're best friends," said Rachel.

"Just like me and Sarah," said Anna, linking little fingers with her sister. "It's great having a big sister."

"I'd love to have a little sister just like you," said Kirsty.

"I'll adopt you for the week," said Anna. "You can all be my big sisters."

There was a knock at the door and Tristan walked in, laughing.

"It sounds as if you're all getting along very well," he said. "I could hear your laughter as I was walking along the path. I'm here to take you to the dining cabin for the introduction."

As Tristan led them all along the winding trail, he told them how much he loved working at the adventure camp.

"The camp directors make everything fun," he said. "They're sisters, just like you, Sarah and Anna."

But when they arrived at the dining cabin, there was an elderly lady standing at the front of the room. A golden trumpet hung on the wall behind her. She was glaring at all the  children and the camp leaders. A scarf was wound around her neck, covering her mouth. A hooked nose curved over it.

"The camp directors have had a quarrel," she croaked. "I'm in charge now, and you all have to do what I say. So keep quiet, do as you're told, and don't bother me."

She turned and stomped through a door labelled 'OFFICE', slamming it shut. Tristan looked shocked.

"The camp directors are more like best friends than sisters," he muttered. "This doesn't make sense."

Tristan hurried off to find out what was happening.

"Why was that lady so grumpy?" asked Anna. "I didn't like her."

Sarah put an arm around her little sister. "Take no notice," she said. "We're together – that's all that matters."

Rachel and Kirsty gave Anna's arm a squeeze. They could see Tristan talking to another camp leader, so they went to try to find out more. The other camp leader's name badge said 'Maria'.

"She even brought her own camp leaders," Maria was saying. "She won't tell us what her plans are for the week. I wish the normal camp directors would come back."

Tristan put his arm around Maria.

"Maybe she's not as mean as she seems," he said. "But whatever happens, we have to make sure that the children have a wonderful week here."

Maria smiled. "You're right," she said, taking the golden trumpet down from the wall. "Let's do what we do best."

She blew a long blast on the trumpet, and everyone turned to listen.

"This is the golden trumpet that gives the camp its name," Maria said. "Whenever you hear one long blast on the trumpet, it will mean that you have to come to the dining cabin. Now, please head back to your cabins and find the map of the camp. Your challenge is to find your way to the ruined castle in the forest for a getting-to-know-you game."

Maria put the trumpet back on the wall. The other children cheered and

dashed out, but Kirsty put her hand on
Rachel's arm.

"The trumpet is glowing," she
whispered. "It looks like …"

"… magic," said Rachel, smiling as she
finished her best friend's sentence.

As the last person left the cabin, Rachel
and Kirsty ran to the trumpet. Kirsty

lifted it down from the wall, and a
shining fairy fluttered out.

"Hello, Kirsty and Rachel!" she said.
"I'm Susie the Sister Fairy."

A Shocking Surprise

"It's wonderful to meet you both at last," said Susie. "I've heard so much about you from the other fairies."

"We're so happy to meet you too," said Rachel. "But what brings you here?"

"Jack Frost, of course," said Susie with a deep sigh. "You see, my job is to make sure that the magical bond between all sisters is strong and true. But this

morning, my magical objects disappeared
– and so did Jack Frost. Queen Titania
asked me to visit you and ask for your
help. There's not much time left."

"What do you mean?" Kirsty asked.

"I've organised a surprise birthday
party for Lila and Myla the Twins
Fairies," Susie explained. "I wanted to

celebrate sisterhood, but everything I've planned will be ruined if I don't get my magical objects back."

"Could you delay the party until we've found Jack Frost?" Rachel suggested.

"It's not just about the party," said Susie. "Without my objects, sisters all over the fairy and human worlds will fall out and turn against each other. But I have no idea where to start looking."

"What are your magical objects?" Kirsty asked. "And what do they do?"

"The dazzling diary planner helps sisters to always make time for each other," said Susie. "The magical padlock helps keep them loyal to each other, and the marvellous mobile phone helps sisters everywhere to feel able to express their thoughts and feelings."

"We'll help you find them," said Kirsty. "We'll think of something."

Susie gave a smile of relief and flitted up to Kirsty's shoulder.

"I'll hide under a lock of your hair," she said. "Thank you, both. I feel better just knowing I'll have your help."

The girls raced back to Maple Cabin, expecting to find Sarah and Anna poring over the map together. But when they burst in, Sarah was glaring at the map and Anna was looking grumpy, with her arms folded across her chest.

"Is everything OK?" asked Kirsty.

"Fine," Sarah snapped. "I'm just checking the map to work out how to get to the ruined castle. Anna's being silly."

"She promised that we would play a game *here*," wailed Anna.

"I forgot," said Sarah, shrugging her shoulders. "There's no time – we have to go to the games in the forest. Besides, *I* thought that we were going to read stories to each other this evening, but now Anna's arranged to meet some new friends in the camp games room instead."

"I changed my mind," said Anna.

Kirsty and Rachel shared a worried glance.

"Let's all go to the forest," said Rachel. "Maybe the game will cheer everyone up."

Sarah went first, using the map to lead them along a wide trail towards the ruined castle. Anna walked behind her, followed by Rachel and Kirsty.

"It's horrible to see Sarah and Anna bickering," said Kirsty.

"I think it's because the dazzling diary planner is missing," Rachel said.

"You're right," said Susie from her hiding place on Kirsty's shoulder. "Sisters everywhere are forgetting their plans and being too busy for each other. I feel so helpless when things go wrong."

Suddenly the trail opened out in front of a crumbling old castle in the middle of the forest. All the camp leaders were there, and Rachel and Kirsty saw Tristan talking to another camp leader called Cameron.

"Have you met the new camp leaders?" the girls heard Cameron ask.

"Not really," said Tristan. "I don't think they're very well. They all looked green when I saw them."

"They don't wear shoes," said Cameron. "And this is going to sound strange, but they all have really enormous feet."

Rachel and Kirsty exchanged horrified glances. Suddenly, everything made sense.

"Oh, Rachel, the new camp leaders are goblins," said Kirsty in a shocked whisper. "Which means that the camp director must be ... *Jack Frost in disguise!*"

Gabbling Goblins

"OK, listen up, everyone," said Tristan, leaping on to a rock. "Hide somewhere in the ruins, and I will be the first seeker. When I find someone, they have to shout out their name and become a seeker until everyone has been found. Ready or not, here I come!"

Everyone scattered. Rachel and Kirsty scooted into the ruins of a tower.

"Do you think the old lady really was Jack Frost in disguise?" Kirsty asked in a whisper.

"If it was him, we know where to start searching for Susie's magical objects," Rachel whispered. "He must have them here at the camp."

"Why would he have taken them?" asked Kirsty. "And why is he running an adventure camp?"

Neither of them knew the answers. As they stared at each other, they heard shouts and squeals as more people were found.

"Let's start searching for the goblins as soon as we're found," said Rachel.

They heard someone scrambling over the fallen stones outside the tower, and then a cheerful face peered in.

"Found you!" Tristan called out.

The girls shouted out their names, and then ran off to start searching. By now, lots of people had been found. Camp leaders and children were running all over the ruins, but there were no goblins to be seen.

"If you were a goblin, where would you hide?" Kirsty asked, looking around.

"Goblins don't like to do as they're told," said Rachel. "We were told to hide in the ruins, so they are sure to be somewhere else."

The girls looked around, and then
Kirsty pointed to a big tree a little
distance from the ruin.

"I thought I saw that tree shaking," she
said.

"But there's not even a breeze," said
Rachel.

"Let's investigate," Susie whispered.

The girls ran over to the tree and peered around it. On the other side of the thick trunk were five goblins in camp leader uniforms. They were pushing each other and squabbling in loud voices.

"Get out of my hiding place," the tallest goblin said, shoving the others away. "I was here first."

"I'll tell Jack Frost on you," said a goblin with a wart on his nose.

"Don't bother Jack Frost," said a goblin with a very deep voice. "He's busy thinking up ways to get his own back on the Rainbow Fairies, for spoiling his plans on Rainspell Island."

"He's already done that, you idiot," said the tall goblin. "He stole Susie the Sister Fairy's magical objects. The Rainbow Fairies are all sisters, so without Susie's objects, they will start squabbling and refuse to work together on anything."

"I thought he took them so he could get rid of the sisters who run this camp," said a goblin with a sparkly heart drawn on his face.

"That was the other reason," said the tall goblin, nodding. "He wants it for all the goblin children who are on holiday at the moment. They're too noisy, so he wants to bring them here so he can get some peace. We just have to drive the humans away first."

"I wish he hadn't brought Jilly Chilly back," said a red-nosed goblin, wiping his nose with the back of his hand. "She gives me the shivers."

"He thinks he can get on with her now he's got that silly fairy's things," said the tall goblin.

"I think she's scary," said the warty goblin.

Rachel and Kirsty hadn't heard Jilly Chilly's name since their adventure with Frances the Royal Family Fairy. Jack Frost had used Frances' magic to create a little sister for himself, but she had annoyed him and he sent her away.

"Why are we playing this stupid game?" asked the deep-voiced goblin. "We're supposed to be burying the *you-know-what* in the forest."

The girls gave each other excited looks. Why had Jack Frost brought Jilly Chilly back now? And what exactly could the goblins be burying?

The You-Know-What

"I don't want to do the digging," whined the tallest goblin. "I don't want to get my new uniform all dirty."

There was a squawking chorus of voices agreeing with him.

"I bet that the 'you-know-what' is one of my magical objects," said Susie.

"I've got an idea," said Kirsty, pulling Rachel a few steps away from the tree. "Susie, if you can turn one of us into a goblin, we could offer to bury the package for them. They might give it to us to save their uniforms."

"I'll do it," said Rachel at once.

Susie waved her wand and a dazzling spark of magic zoomed out and landed on Rachel's head. She started to turn green from the head down. Her nose and ears grew, her hair disappeared and she was suddenly wearing an adventure camp leader's uniform.

"Good luck," Kirsty whispered.

Rachel cleared her throat, stepped around the tree and put her hands on her hips.

"Why haven't you buried that package yet?" she said in her grumpiest voice.

"Jack Frost could turn up any minute, and then we'd all be in trouble."

The goblins all started arguing at once. There was a clamour of goblin squawks about uniforms and mud.

"I'll do it," Rachel said, as loudly as she could. "Give me the you-know-what. I'll bury it."

The tallest goblin shoved a brown paper package into her hands and she turned away. Then she heard the warty goblin's voice.

"I thought there were only five of us at the camp," he said.

"But there are five of us standing here," said another goblin in a shocked voice. "So who's *that*?"

Rachel didn't wait to hear any more. She sprinted into the wood as fast as her green legs could carry her. Behind her, she heard the thump of running goblin feet. As she ran, she tore the paper off the parcel and saw that it was a glimmering diary.

"Get her!" shouted a voice.

Rachel gasped as she felt a hand grab her from behind, and then she saw Susie zooming in front of her.

She flung the diary
up as hard as she
could, and Susie
caught it in mid-
air. The goblins
screeched, but the
diary instantly
shrank to
fairy size.
Then
Susie
waved her
wand to
turn Rachel
back into a
human, and the goblins screeched again.

"You pesky, interfering little human!"
they all squawked in fury, shaking their
fists at Rachel.

"Leave my best friend alone," panted Kirsty, racing up behind them.

"We're going to tell Jack Frost and Jilly Chilly," the goblins retorted. "You'll be sorry for this."

They ran off, and Kirsty and Rachel hugged each other. Susie swooped down and hovered in front of them, her eyes sparkling.

"It's my dazzling diary planner," she said, hugging it to her chest. "I can't believe I've got it back – thank you both so much. I must take it back to Fairyland straight away."

"Come back soon," said Rachel. "We won't stop looking until we've found all your magical objects."

Smiling, Susie waved her wand and disappeared in a puff of silver fairy dust. Rachel and Kirsty raced each other back to the ruined castle. The first people they saw were Sarah and Anna, holding hands and giggling as they searched together.

"I guess that when you have a sister, you always have someone to play with," said Kirsty, watching them.

Rachel took her hand and squeezed it.

"Guess what?" she said. "It's exactly the same when you have a best friend."

Kirsty grinned at her.

"Come on then, Rachel," she said. "Let's go and enjoy the biggest game of hide-and-seek *ever!*"

The Magical
Padlock

Contents

Chapter Six: A Sad Sister   65

Chapter Seven: Fairies Fall Out   75

Chapter Eight: Pretend Party   85

Chapter Nine: A Light Bulb Moment   97

Chapter Ten: Sisters' Snap!   107

A Sad Sister

"It's already our second day at the camp," said Rachel. "We have to try to find out more about what Jack Frost is doing here."

Rachel and Kirsty's first day at Golden Trumpet Adventure Camp had been very exciting. They had met their new friends

Anna and Sarah. They had helped Susie
the Sister Fairy to get one of her magical
objects back from the goblins. And they
had found out that Jack Frost was in
disguise as the camp's new director. After
a cosy night's sleep in Maple Cabin,
they had spent the morning horse-riding
with Anna and Sarah. Now they were
sitting on the edge of the jetty that jutted
out into Sparkle Lake. This was the first
moment they had had a
chance to talk about
Jack Frost or Susie
the Sister Fairy's
missing magical
objects.

Kirsty swung
her legs back
and forth. She and

Rachel were waiting for Tristan to give them their first waterskiing lesson. The other two children in their group were having their lesson, which gave the girls time to chat about their adventures so far.

"Yes, we have to help Susie and stop Jack Frost and Jilly Chilly causing trouble," Kirsty agreed. "I wonder when we'll see Susie again."

"We haven't got anything to tell her yet," said Rachel. "We haven't seen Jack Frost or the goblins since we got the dazzling diary planner back."

"Jack Frost knows we're here now," said Kirsty. "That's why he keeps himself locked in the camp director's office. He'll be trying to make it impossible for us to find the other missing objects."

"Well, we can't do anything until we see Susie again," said Rachel, leaning back to let the sunshine warm her face. "In the meantime, there is so much to do here!"

At that moment, Tristan's boat sped past, pulling the other two children in their group along on waterskis. Rachel and Kirsty waved, feeling excited that it

would soon be their turn. A footstep on the jetty behind them made them turn around. They saw Anna walking slowly towards them. As she got closer, they could see that her eyes were red and her face was blotchy.

"You've been crying," Kirsty exclaimed, jumping to her feet. "What's wrong?"

"Sarah is being really mean to me," said Anna in between sniffs. "She's told the other girls that I'm scared of balloons, and they've all been laughing about it."

69

Rachel and Kirsty exchanged a surprised glance. This didn't sound like Sarah, who loved Anna very much.

"Perhaps she didn't know it would upset you so much," said Rachel in a gentle voice. "I'm sure she wouldn't hurt your feelings on purpose."

"It's her dream to be a ballet dancer," Anna went on. "She has been having dancing lessons to surprise Mum and Dad, and I haven't told anyone. But now she's been so horrid to me, I'm going to phone home and spoil her surprise. I'll never tell her anything again."

Anna stomped off, and the girls groaned at exactly the same time.

"This has happened because Susie's magical padlock is missing," said Kirsty. "Anna shouldn't even be telling *us* about Sarah's dancing – let alone her parents."

"You're right," said Rachel. "Susie told us that without the padlock, sisters wouldn't be loyal to each other. Now Anna and Sarah are telling things about each other that they shouldn't. It's awful, and we have to do something about it."

"As soon as we see Susie again, we will put it all right," Kirsty said in a determined voice.

The roar of Tristan's speedboat made them turn, and they waved as he pulled up alongside them, grinning.

"Ready for your lesson?" he asked as the other children scrambled on to the jetty.

Rachel and Kirsty nodded. They could hardly wait!

Fairies Fall Out

Feeling excited, Rachel and Kirsty pulled on their life jackets.

"Remember what I told you earlier," said Tristan. "If you want to go over to the nearest jetty, pat your head. If you want me to stop the boat, bring your hand to your neck. If I'm going to turn the boat, I will put my finger in the air

and circle it around. Now, pull your knees
up to your chests. The life jackets will
hold you up in the water."

Rachel and Kirsty followed his
instructions, and soon they were bobbing
in the water with their ski tips pointing
up in front of them. There were two ropes
attached to the back of the boat, and the
girls held on to them with both hands.

"Keep your arms straight," said Tristan,
starting the engine.

He moved the boat away slowly,
and the girls let it pull them out of the
water and up on to their skis. The ropes
tightened.

"My
legs feel
wobbly,"
said
Rachel with
a giggle.

"Tristan
said that we
should keep
them bent, remember?" said Kirsty.

The boat moved faster, and suddenly
they were whooshing along on the
water. Their hearts thumped. The spray
soon drenched their hair, and the wind
whipped it out of their eyes.

"This feels amazing!" Kirsty shouted.

Tristan kept glancing back at them over his shoulder, checking that they were OK.

They were going around the lake for a second time when Kirsty saw something glimmering at the edge of the lake, close to another jetty.

There was no time to ask Rachel.

Kirsty knew that she had to make a
decision straight
away. She
patted her
head, and
Tristan saw
her at once.
He steered
the boat over
to the jetty
and drew the girls
along after him.

"What's happening?" Rachel asked.

"I'll explain in a minute," Kirsty said.
"Just go along with whatever I say, OK?"

Rachel nodded. As always, she trusted
her best friend completely. Tristan leaned
over the back of the boat and gazed
down at them bobbing in the water.

"Are you both OK?" Tristan asked.

"We're fine, and that was brilliant fun!" said Kirsty. "But I've suddenly thought of something we have to do right now. Is it OK if we leave here and head back up to the dining cabin?"

"No problem," said Tristan. "I'll go back and give the others another turn."

He waited to make sure that they were safely out of the water, and then zoomed back across the lake. As soon as he had gone, Rachel hopped from foot to foot in excitement.

"What's happened?" she asked. "Did you see a goblin or Jack Frost? Or did you spot something magical?"

Kirsty grinned and parted the bushes in front of them. Susie was inside, sitting cross-legged and smiling at them.

"It's wonderful to see you again so soon," said Rachel. "Have you come to look for your other missing magical objects?"

Susie nodded and fluttered up to perch on a twig.

"I've been busy getting ready for Lila and Myla's party," she said. "It's not going very well. The Rainbow Fairies are supposed to be helping me, but they have stopped sharing their ideas with each other, and they have been telling the rest of us private things that we are not supposed to know. It's not how sisters are meant to act. Now they have all stopped helping me to get the party ready. They say that they won't carry on if their sisters are helping. If I don't get my magical padlock back soon, the whole surprise will be spoiled."

"Oh no it won't," said Kirsty. "We're not going to let that happen, are we, Rachel?"

"Definitely not," said Rachel. "But how can we stop Jack Frost?"

Pretend Party

"I've had an idea," said Susie. "Will you let me turn you into fairies so that we can search here at the camp? We will have a better chance of looking in all the nooks and crannies if you can fly like me."

Rachel and Kirsty nodded, feeling the rush of excitement that always came when they were about to get fairy wings.

Susie raised her wand, and two sparkling ribbons of fairy dust curled out of the tip. One of the ribbons was gold and the other was silver. The silver one wound around Rachel's waist like a shining belt, and the gold one did the same to Kirsty. The girls were lifted into the air, and as they shrank to fairy size, their filmy wings appeared. Then the magical belts disappeared in a puff of glittering magic. Susie flew over to hover beside Rachel and Kirsty.

"Where shall we start looking?" she asked.

"How about trying the camp director's office?" said Rachel.

"But it's always locked," said Kirsty. "Tristan was saying earlier that he hasn't seen the new camp director at all. Every since he found out we were here, Jack Frost has been sending out his orders through the goblin camp leaders – and Jilly Chilly, of course."

Rachel shivered. She wasn't looking forward to seeing Jack Frost's bad-tempered sister again.

"We need to think of a way to get him out of his office," she said. "Then we can search for the padlock."

"How about making something interesting happen in another part of the camp?" Kirsty said. "Jack Frost doesn't like missing out on anything. When he comes out of his office to see what's happening, we can slip inside."

"That's a brilliant idea," said Rachel, clapping her hands together. "Let's go."

The three fairies zoomed high into the blue sky, and flew over the camp towards the dining cabin at the centre. Looking down, they could see the adventure camp laid out below them like a map.

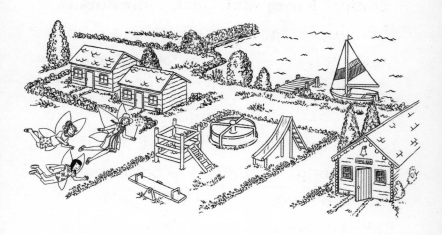

"There's the big climbing wall," Kirsty said, spotting the enormous cream wall with its colourful foot and hand holds. "And there's the stable where we went horse-riding this morning."

"That must have been lots of fun," said Susie. "How about organising a horse-riding lesson for Jack Frost?"

"I can't imagine Jack Frost on a horse," said Rachel. "I don't think he'd enjoy it very much. What about setting off a fire alarm? If he thinks there's a fire at the camp, he would have to come out."

"He wouldn't care about that unless it was in his office," said Susie with a sigh. "Jack Frost doesn't care about anyone except himself."

"What about a party?" said Kirsty. "We know that he loves parties, and he wouldn't want to miss out on party games and food."

"Good thinking," said Susie. "Look, there's the dining cabin."

"The office is inside the cabin," said Rachel.

There was no one around to see them swoop into the dining cabin through the open door.

They hovered
on either side
of the office
door and
listened.
They could
hear a
screeching
voice coming
from inside the
room.

"That's Jilly Chilly," Kirsty whispered.

"I want this place to change right
now," Jilly Chilly was shouting. "There
are too many children here and I'm sick
of hearing them giggling and yelling
all the time. Why won't the goblins do
as they're told? Why do I have to keep
saying the same things over and over and

over again? Let's get rid of all the stupid
visitors and fill the place with goblins.
Then we can go back to the Ice Castle
and have some peace."

"Goodness, I bet Jack Frost is cross that
she's doing all the talking," said Rachel
in a low voice. "He isn't getting a word
in edgeways."

"Let's start talking about a party," said
Susie. "As soon as the
office is empty, we
can search for the
padlock."

"You mean
that amazing
party at the
climbing wall?"
asked Kirsty, raising her
voice as loud as she could.

"With all the cakes and pies and jelly and ice cream?"

Rachel grinned at her.

"Yes, it's the best party I've ever been to," she said. "I can't decide which game is best – pass the parcel or musical chairs or pin the tail on the donkey."

"I heard that there are some *amazing* prizes," Susie added.

Suddenly, they heard chairs scraping on the floor inside the room.

"They're coming," Rachel whispered. "It's time to hide!"

A Light Bulb Moment

The three fairies shot out of sight behind
the golden trumpet that hung on the
wall. They were just in the nick of time,
for seconds later the office door was
flung open. Jack Frost sprinted out, still
in his disguise of a wig, a flowery dress
and a cape. Jilly Chilly was behind him,
looking meaner than ever with her sharp

nose and sulky expression. Three goblins
capered out of the office after her.

"This is our chance," Kirsty whispered.
She, Rachel and Susie flew into the
office, just before the last goblin slammed
the door shut.

"Lock the door, you nincompoop!" they
heard Jack Frost bellow.

The key turned in the lock, and the fairies exchanged worried glances.

"I hope we can find the magical padlock before Jack Frost realises he's been tricked and comes back," said Rachel. "Let's start looking."

The great padlock search began. The fairies hunted through cupboards and rummaged in drawers. They scoured shelves and peered underneath chairs and cushions. They checked inside every  vase and peeped behind every picture.

But the magical padlock was nowhere to be seen.

"Nothing," said Susie, sinking on to the desk with a groan.

Rachel and Kirsty fluttered down and put their arms around her shoulders.

"Maybe it isn't in here after all," said Kirsty. "Don't be sad, Susie. I promise that we will keep looking until we find it."

"Where would Jack Frost hide something like a magical padlock?" Rachel murmured.

Just then, they heard the thump of big

feet on the wooden floor of the cabin.
The squawk of goblin voices grew louder,
and then they were drowned out by Jack
Frost's furious screech.

"You idiots!" he roared. "Where did the
party go? It's all your fault!"

The three fairies looked around the
room in a panic. Where could they hide?
The windows were all shut and there was
no escape.

"We'll have to hover against the ceiling," said Rachel. "We've done it before — we just have to hope that no one looks up."

She glanced up as she spoke, and stared in wonder. The ceiling light was a bowl made of glass, and something metallic was glinting inside the bowl.

"Look!' Rachel cried.

The three fairies zoomed up to the light and slid into the bowl of the lampshade. As the key turned in the door, Susie reached out and touched her glimmering magical

padlock. It instantly shrank to fairy size,
and she hugged it to her chest.

"Thank you," she whispered as the
door opened. "You have made everything
right."

Rachel and Kirsty didn't dare to reply.
They had to be completely silent. But
they forgot to keep their wings still,
and the light sent strange, wing-shaped
shadows fluttering around the room. Jack
Frost looked up.

"No!" he shouted. "You pesky, interfering, silly little fairies!"

Susie, Rachel and Kirsty flew out of the lampshade, and Jack Frost pulled out his wand and pointed it at them.

"You're not taking that padlock," he said. "Give it back or else!"

"Never," said Kirsty.

"Get them!" Jilly Chilly screeched.

Jack Frost sent a lightning bolt hurtling towards the fairies.

Sisters' Snap!

The fairies dived out of the way, and the lightning bolt hit the light. The glass shattered and rained down on the desk. The goblins started squawking and wailing.

"Get them!" Jilly Chilly howled. "Squash them! Stop them!"

Jack Frost leaped on to the desk, waving his wand around wildly. Blue flashes pinged around the room and the goblins dived for cover.

"I have to get us out of here," Susie cried. "*To Fairyland without delay, whisk me and my two friends away!*"

She gave her
wand a fast
flick, and the
office instantly
disappeared
in a mass of
shimmering
sparkles. Rachel
and Kirsty
blinked a few
times. When
the sparkles
disappeared, they

saw they were standing in a fairy glade.
In front of them, a 'Happy Birthday'
banner was drooping down from a tree,
waiting to be strung up. Party decorations
were lying on the grass, and party tables
were still waiting for coloured tablecloths

to make them look jolly. Several fairies were sitting around on the grass, all with very glum expressions. They glanced up at Susie, who didn't say a word. She simply held up the magical padlock.

"Hurray!" The fairies sprang to their feet, all sad expressions gone. They cheered and danced around, laughing and smiling. Then one of them pointed into the distance.

"It's the Rainbow Fairies!" said Rachel.

"They're friends again."

All seven of the fairy sisters were zooming towards them, flying hand in hand.

"Now we can really get ready for the birthday party," said Susie, a smile lighting up her face. "The only thing that's missing is the marvellous mobile."

"Susie, please send us back to the adventure camp," said Kirsty. "We want to start looking for clues as soon as we can."

"But could you return us to our cabin?" Rachel said, as Susie raised her wand. "We don't want to end up back in Jack Frost's office!"

Laughing, Susie waved her wand and the girls were wrapped in a cloud of magical sparkles. When the sparkles faded, they were standing in front of the door to their cabin. They hurried inside and saw Anna and Sarah hugging each other.

"Is everything OK?" Rachel asked
at once. "We were worried about you
earlier."

"Everything's fine now," said Anna with
a happy smile.

"It wasn't very nice for a while," Sarah
added. "I'm not sure what happened. But
the wonderful thing about sisters is that
we will always forgive each other."

"We were just going to play a game of snap," said Anna. "Do you want to join in?"

Soon, all four girls were shrieking with laughter as they plunked down their cards. Just before taking her next turn, Sarah paused and gazed around at Rachel and Kirsty.

"You two are just as close as sisters, aren't you?" she said.

"I think so," said Kirsty, smiling at Rachel. "The more I learn about having a sister, the more I see how much like sisters we are!"

The Marvellous
Mobile

Contents

Chapter Eleven: Goblins and Obstacles 121

Chapter Twelve: Cargo Capers 129

Chapter Thirteen: The Golden Ladder 139

Chapter Fourteen: Searching Spell 149

Chapter Fifteen: The New Camp 161

Goblins and Obstacles

"I've never been on an obstacle course like this before," said Kirsty.

"Are you nervous?" Rachel asked.

"A little bit," said Kirsty. "But it looks like lots of fun."

It was their third day at Golden Trumpet Adventure Camp, and the camp leaders had told everyone to meet at the bird-watching hut in the centre of the forest. They were at the start of a huge obstacle course and Tristan was counting everyone to make sure they were all there.

Just then, Jilly Chilly walked past with her goblin camp leaders.

"Keep an eye on those annoying humans," she hissed to them. "Don't let them out of your sight."

Rachel and Kirsty exchanged an alarmed glance.

"Today we're going to have a wild adventure," said Tristan, jumping up on to a tree stump so that everyone could see him. "There are zip wires, cargo nets, ladders, wobbly logs ... everything you can imagine. Are you ready for it?"

"YES!" shouted the crowd of children.

Suddenly, Jilly Chilly shoved him aside.

"You are probably all going to get this completely wrong," she said. "Copy what my camp leaders are doing, and don't act like complete fools."

Tristan frowned and spoke again.

"We're going to split you into two teams," he said. "The winners will be the team that reaches the dining cabin first."

He and the other human camp leaders started dividing everyone up, and Rachel and Kirsty found themselves in the same team as Sarah. Anna was in the other team.

"There's no sign of Susie so far," said Rachel. "Let's start the obstacle challenge and find out as much as we can about the camp. Maybe something will give us a clue about where the marvellous mobile could be."

Their team's first challenge was the zip wire. Tristan was there, and Kirsty leaned over to whisper in Rachel's ear.

"Now's our chance to find out something about how the camp is run," she said.

Rachel nodded and smiled at Tristan.

"This seems like a fun place to work," she said.

"It is," said Tristan, nodding, and then his smile faded.

"Well, it used to be.

Things are a bit different now that the new camp directors are in charge."

"Do you wish that the old camp directors would come back?" Kirsty asked.

"I've visited them with some of the other camp leaders," said Tristan in a low voice. "They're

sisters, so we thought they would have made up by now and maybe we could get them to come back. But every time they talk to each other, they argue and fall out. It's really sad, because they used to be best friends."

But just then, Rachel and Kirsty had to stop asking questions.

"Oh my goodness," said Kirsty, biting her lip. "It's our turn on the zip wire!"

Cargo Capers

Kirsty was a bit nervous, but Tristan
patted her on the back.

"It isn't very high," he said. "You can
waterski, and that's much harder. This
will be a breeze!"

Feeling better, Kirsty took a deep
breath and set off down the wire. Rachel
was close behind her.

"I think that the old camp directors must be falling out because of the missing magical mobile, don't you?" called Rachel as they whizzed along.

Susie had told them that the marvellous mobile helped sisters to express what they thought and how they felt. Without it, the camp directors were not able to understand each other.

"If only we could find out where

Jack Frost has hidden the mobile, then everything would return to normal here and in the fairy world," Kirsty called back over her shoulder. Before Rachel could reply, she heard jeering laughter. She looked to her right and saw that there was another zip wire there, running alongside the one she and Kirsty were on. The five camp-leader goblins were whizzing along it in a row, far too close together.

"You'll never find the phone!" one of them squawked.

"Give up and go home!" shouted another.

"You'll never beat Jack Frost and Jilly Chilly," a third goblin shouted. "They're going to make this a goblin camp and there's nothing you can do about it!"

Cackling with laughter, the goblins didn't notice that they were reaching the end of the zip wire. WHUMP! The first one had just landed on the ground when the other four came crashing into the back of him.

Rachel and Kirsty jumped down from their zip wire and hurried on to the next obstacle, leaving the goblins in a tangle of bony arms and legs.

"We know that the mobile's not in Jack Frost's office because we've already searched that," said Rachel as they clambered up the cargo net side by side. "Oh, Kirsty, what if he's carrying it in his pocket?"

The cargo net suddenly started jumping around, and the girls looked down. The five goblins had finally untangled themselves and were now climbing up behind them.

"Ooh, I don't like this," the smallest one wailed. "The rope feels funny between my toes. I've got sensitive feet!"

"Stop moaning," said a goblin with a warty nose, giving him a shove.

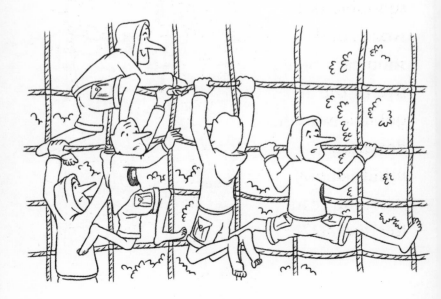

The first goblin tumbled backwards and dangled upside down, his enormous feet caught in the ropes.

"Now look what you've done," said a third goblin.

He shoved the one with the warty nose, who lost his grip and fell sideways, his arms and legs dangling through the holes. The squabble got worse, and soon all five of the goblins were dangling upside down, struggling to free themselves.

"I hope Jack Frost finds that stupid mobile soon, so we can all stop looking," screeched the warty goblin.

Rachel and Kirsty shared a look of astonishment.

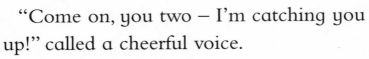

"Surely Jack Frost *has* the mobile?" said Kirsty. "Why would he need the goblins to be looking for it?"

"Come on, you two – I'm catching you up!" called a cheerful voice.

It was Tristan, and he was climbing up the net behind them. But when he saw the goblins were stuck, he stopped to help them. Grinning, the girls hurried over the rest of the net and then jogged towards the next obstacle – the swaying bridge.

Just before they got there, they felt sharp elbows knocking them sideways into a bush. It was the goblins!

The Golden Ladder

The goblins sprinted past Rachel and
Kirsty, laughing at them as they struggled
out of the bush. Tristan came along and
helped them up. He looked very cross
with the goblins.

"Terrible manners," he said. "That's
not how camp leaders are supposed to

behave. I'm going to have a word with them."

He hurried on as Sarah came along by herself.

"This is fun," she said.

But she didn't look very happy. Rachel and Kirsty linked arms with her.

"I'm sorry you don't have Anna with you," said Rachel. "It's a shame that she was put in the other team."

"I don't mind," Sarah replied.

"Normally I can tell Anna anything, but since we arrived here, everything seems different between us. It isn't easy to tell her about how I feel any more. She just misunderstands everything."

"I'm sure things will be back to normal soon," said Kirsty.

Sarah shrugged. "I don't know," she said. "It must be because she's younger than me. Maybe it will never be the same between us again."

She went ahead to the swaying bridge, but Rachel and Kirsty did not run after her. They both felt sad and worried.

"This is all because of the missing mobile," said Rachel.

"We have to get it back for sisters like Sarah and Anna," Kirsty said. "We can't let Jack Frost win."

The girls stepped onto the swaying
bridge. It was made of rope, with a single
plank of wood to walk along. As soon as
they stepped on to it, they felt it swinging
from side to side. It was
hard to keep their
balance as
they walked
along,
slowly
placing
one foot
in front of
the other.

"Look up ahead," said Rachel suddenly.
She was in front, and she had noticed a
single goblin camp leader standing in the
middle of the bridge. As they got closer,
they saw that he looked terrified. It was

the smallest one, who had complained about looking for the mobile. He was quivering all over.

"Don't be scared," said Rachel, gently taking his hand. "You can do it."

"It's easy," Kirsty added. "Just trust us and don't look down."

"Now," said Rachel. "Lift your left foot and take one little step forwards."

Tiny step by tiny step, the girls guided the goblin to the other side of the bridge. At last, still quivering, he stepped on to solid ground again.

"I did it!" he yelled.

He tried to dart away, but Rachel had her hand around his wrist.

"Not so fast," she said. "If you can't be polite enough to say thank you, at least  you can tell us what has happened to the marvellous mobile."

The goblin glared at her.

"It doesn't matter if you know," he said. "It won't help you. Jack Frost hid the mobile somewhere in the camp, but he has forgotten where. So we have to hunt for it day and night. I'm fed up with this camp. Now leave me alone!"

He ran off and the girls stared at each other.

"Is this good news or not?" Kirsty asked, puzzled.

Behind them, the rest of the camp
leaders were hurrying across the bridge.
Suddenly, Rachel saw something
glimmering among the trees to her right.

She stepped a little closer, and saw a
golden ladder disappearing up into the
canopy of trees.

"Is that part of the obstacle course?" she asked, feeling unsure.

"I don't think so," said Kirsty, sounding excited. "It's sparkling with fairy dust!"

Searching Spell

Rachel and Kirsty sprinted over to the ladder and started to climb up into the tree's branches. The thick leaves soon hid them from the eyes of the camp leaders below. At the top they found Susie hovering and smiling at them.

"Oh, Susie, we've got some news," said Kirsty, clambering on to a branch so that

Rachel could see the little fairy. "Jack Frost has lost your marvellous mobile phone. He hid it and now he can't remember where it is."

Susie clapped her hands together.

"That's wonderful news," she said. "Now my mobile is not stolen, but lost. That means I can use a special spell to find lost things."

She lifted her wand above her head.

"Fairy magic, hear my plea.
Jack Frost has stolen things from me.
One object's lost, its place unknown.

Please take me to my magical phone!"

A tiny light, like a firefly, shot from the tip of her wand and hovered above her head. Susie waved her wand and fairy dust sprinkled on to the girls, transforming them into fairies. They rose into the air, fluttering their wings in delight at being able to fly again.

"Come on!" cried Susie.

The little light went dancing and darting into the forest, spinning and swirling around the trees and swooping under bushes.

The fairies followed it, while the laughter of the children and the camp leaders on the obstacle course echoed through the forest.

"It's like the wildest rollercoaster ride ever!" squealed Rachel as the light looped and twirled.

At last it dived down to a tuft of grass at the very edge of the forest, a few steps from the dining cabin. It hovered above the grass, shining like a beacon, and the fairies rushed towards it.

"Not so fast!"

It was Jack Frost, still disguised as an elderly lady. He leapt out in front of them, followed by Jilly Chilly, and plunged his hand into the tuft of grass.

"Got it!" he shrieked, holding up the marvellous mobile phone. "Thanks for finding it for me, silly fairies!"

"Now we can make sure that those daft camp directors never come back," added Jilly Chilly. "They'll be too busy arguing with each other to worry about what's happening here.

We can drive the humans out and bring the goblin children in!"

Jack Frost scowled and flapped his scarf at her.

"Stop interrupting me!" he snapped. "That's what *I* was about to say!"

Kirsty fluttered forward. Even though Jack Frost was scary, she couldn't bear the thought of Sarah and Anna not being friends any more.

"Your plan will never work," she told
Jack Frost. "The camp is not set up for
goblin children. There is nothing here
they like! They won't be happy and
they'll go home, being noisier than ever.
If you want to keep them happy, you
should build them a special park of their
own, not steal one that belongs to other
people."

Jack Frost
glared at
her, but he
didn't say
anything.

"She's
right," said
Rachel, coming
to hover beside

155

Kirsty. "It could
have goblin-
sized rides and
everything
could be
painted
green. There
could be a
special climbing
wall with grips for
long, bony fingers."

"It could have a café hut with all the
food that goblins like best, and a games
room with a big dressing-up box," Susie
added. "I could build something like that
in the blink of an eye."

"There could be a little lake with a
goblin-sized ship on it, and paddle boats
with big pedals for goblin feet," said

Kirsty. "You could build it in the woods behind the Ice Castle. You wouldn't have to hear it or even see it."

Jack Frost's eyes were growing wider and wider.

"Could you really make a park like that?" he asked at last.

"Easily, with fairy magic," said Susie. "But only if I have my marvellous mobile phone. I can't do anything without it."

Jilly Chilly had a look of panic on her sharp face.

"Stop listening," she snapped at Jack. "You can't do this. Ignore them and come with me."

Jack Frost turned on her with a growl. "Stop telling me what to do," he hissed.

"I'm not going to be ordered about by my little sister. I'm going to please myself, and you can't stop me!"

The New Camp

Jack Frost ripped off his disguise and shoved the phone towards Susie. She fluttered forward, and as soon as she touched the phone it shrank to fairy size.

"NO!" screamed Jilly Chilly furiously, throwing herself on the ground and hammering the grass with her feet and fists. "No! No! No!"

Susie smiled,
and her wand
seemed to
glow with new
energy. "Now
that I have
my marvellous
mobile back, I
can do something
to help you," she
said to Jack Frost.

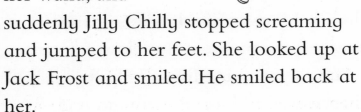

She waved
her wand, and
suddenly Jilly Chilly stopped screaming
and jumped to her feet. She looked up at
Jack Frost and smiled. He smiled back at
her.

"I don't want to argue with you," he
said. "You're my sister."

"I agree," said Jilly Chilly. "These annoying fairies can't get the better of us. Especially with you in charge!"

"Yes," said Jack Frost. "We shouldn't fight with each other. *They're* the ones we should be plotting against."

Susie winked at Rachel and Kirsty, and then waved her wand again. In a flash they were all standing in the woods by the Ice Castle.

"Now," she said, "it's time to put everything right."

Fairy dust exploded from Susie's wand as she magically built an enormous adventure camp before their eyes. Green turrets and cabins rose from the ground, while games and rides grew instantly and a small lake bubbled up from the forest floor, complete with a miniature pirate ship and a row of paddle boats. Then they heard high-pitched squeals, and a crowd of goblin children came racing through the woods towards them. Jilly Chilly and Jack Frost showed them the way in, snapping at them to keep the noise down.

Rachel and Kirsty laughed out loud to see the delight of the little goblins.

"We're just in time for the surprise birthday party," said Susie. "Let's go!"

There was another magical flash, and
the three fairies were transported to the
fairy glade they had seen the day before.
The 'Happy Birthday' banner was
strung between the trees,
party decorations were
draped on every
bush, and the
party tables
were piled high
with cupcakes,
berry bowls,
biscuits, jellies
and tiny triangle
sandwiches. Fairies
filled the space, some sitting
cross-legged on the grass, some
standing and some fluttering in the air.
Then a cry went up. "They're coming!"

A few seconds later, Lila and Myla
appeared, led by the Rainbow Fairies.
They had blindfolds around their
eyes. When Amber and Sky
pulled the blindfolds off,
everyone shouted,
"SURPRISE!"
They all
congratulated
Lila and Myla,
and then the
feast began,
followed by
dancing and party
games. At last Rachel
and Kirsty collapsed on to
the grass, breathless with laughter.
"Pass the parcel should *always* be
played in mid-air," said Rachel.

Kirsty grinned at her, and Susie fluttered over to them.

"It's time for me to send you back to Golden Trumpet Adventure Camp," she said. "Thank you both for everything you've done for me. This party would have been a disaster without you."

"We loved being able to help," said Kirsty.

They all shared a hug, and then Susie waved her wand. In a flurry of sparkles, the girls found themselves standing in the dining cabin once again.

Two ladies were standing at the front,
holding the golden trumpet between
them. They looked very alike.

"They must be the camp directors," said
Rachel in a whisper. "They're back!"

The girls looked around. They could
see Tristan smiling and talking to Maria.
Then they spotted Anna and Sarah with
their arms around each other, chattering
and giggling happily.

"Everything is back to normal," said Kirsty. "Thank goodness."

"We're very glad to be back," one of the directors said. "And we are really looking forward to spending the rest of the week with you. We have some exciting ideas for activities, and we'd love to hear your ideas too. Let's have some fun!"

Everyone cheered, and Rachel and Kirsty shared a hug.

"I've loved every adventure we've had here so far – human and magical," said Rachel. "I can't wait for the next one!"

The End

Now it's time for Kirsty and
Rachel to help...

Debbie the
Duckling Fairy

Read on for a sneak peek...

"It's so nice of your friends to invite
me to the farm with you," said Rachel
Walker.

Her best friend Kirsty Tate smiled. They
were on their way to Greenfields Farm
in the car with Mr and Mrs Tate. The
farm was just outside Wetherbury, Kirsty's
home town, where the two best friends
were spending the spring half-term
holiday.

"Greenfields Farm is so cool," Kirsty
said. "Mum and Dad have known the

owners for years, and they were really happy to invite you along as well."

"Niall and Harriet Hawkins work very hard," said Mr Tate. "They've been planning to open the farm to paying visitors for months."

"They were so happy when we offered to help them set up for the opening at the end of this week," Mrs Tate added.

Read **Debbie the Duckling Fairy** to find out what adventures are in store for Kirsty and Rachel!

RAINBOW magic™

Calling all parents, carers and teachers!
The Rainbow Magic fairies are here to help
your child enter the magical world of reading.
Whatever reading stage they are at, there's
a Rainbow Magic book for everyone!
Here is Lydia the Reading Fairy's guide to
supporting your child's journey at all levels.

Starting Out

1 Our Rainbow Magic Beginner Readers are perfect for first-time readers who are just beginning to develop reading skills and confidence. Approved by teachers, they contain a full range of educational levelling, as well as lively full-colour illustrations.

Developing Readers

2 Rainbow Magic Early Readers contain longer stories and wider vocabulary for building stamina and growing confidence. These are adaptations of our most popular Rainbow Magic stories, specially developed for younger readers in conjunction with an Early Years reading consultant, with full-colour illustrations.

Going Solo

3 The Rainbow Magic chapter books – a mixture of series and one-off specials – contain accessible writing to encourage your child to venture into reading independently. These highly collectible and much-loved magical stories inspire a love of reading to last a lifetime.

www.rainbowmagicbooks.co.uk

"Rainbow Magic got my daughter reading chapter books. Great sparkly covers, cute fairies and traditional stories full of magic that she found impossible to put down" – Mother of Edie (6 years)

"Florence LOVES the Rainbow Magic books. She really enjoys reading now" – Mother of Florence (6 years)

The Rainbow Magic
Reading Challenge

Well done, fairy friend – you have completed the book!
This book was worth 10 points.

See how far you have climbed on the
Reading Rainbow opposite.

The more books you read, the more points you will get,
and the closer you will be to becoming a Fairy Princess!

Do you want your own Reading Rainbow?
1. Cut out the coin below
2. Go to the Rainbow Magic website
3. Download and print out your poster
4. Add your coin and climb up the Reading Rainbow!

There's all this and lots more at
www.rainbowmagicbooks.co.uk

You'll find activities, competitions, stories, a special
newsletter and complete profiles of all the
Rainbow Magic fairies. Find a fairy with your name!